INTERNATIONAL SPACE STATION

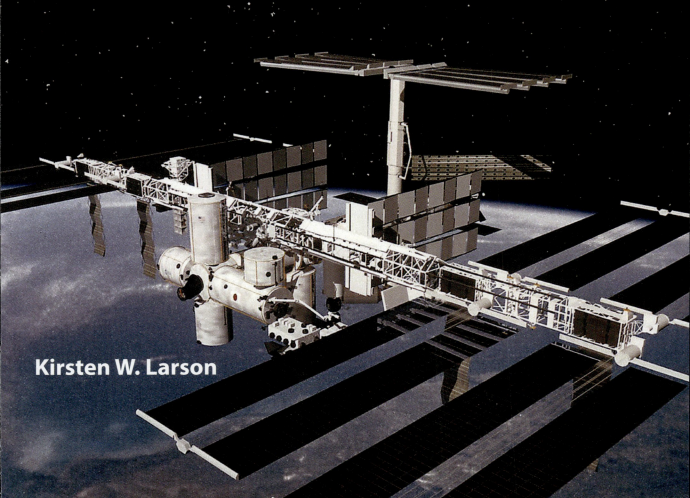

Kirsten W. Larson

Rourke
Educational Media

rourkeeducationalmedia.com

Before & After Reading Activities

Before Reading:

Building Academic Vocabulary and Background Knowledge

Before reading a book, it is important to tap into what your child or students already know about the topic. This will help them develop their vocabulary, increase their reading comprehension, and make connections across the curriculum.

1. *Look at the cover of the book. What will this book be about?*
2. *What do you already know about the topic?*
3. *Let's study the Table of Contents. What will you learn about in the book's chapters?*
4. *What would you like to learn about this topic? Do you think you might learn about it from this book? Why or why not?*
5. *Use a reading journal to write about your knowledge of this topic. Record what you already know about the topic and what you hope to learn about the topic.*
6. *Read the book.*
7. *In your reading journal, record what you learned about the topic and your response to the book.*
8. *After reading the book complete the activities below.*

Content Area Vocabulary
Read the list. What do these words mean?
atmosphere
cosmonauts
dehydrated
GPS
insulation
meteorites
microgravity
orbits
radiation
stress

After Reading:

Comprehension and Extension Activity

After reading the book, work on the following questions with your child or students in order to check their level of reading comprehension and content mastery.

1. *What are some things engineers must consider when building in space? (Summarize)*
2. *What are some of the different pieces that make up the International Space Station? (Asking Questions)*
3. *If you could live in space, would you? (Text to Self Connection)*
4. *Who put together the ISS in space, and how did they do it? (Asking Questions)*
5. *What are some reasons to have a space station? (Asking Questions)*

Extension Activity

Design your own space station! What types of rooms will you need? What should they be shaped like? What jobs will your space station do?

TABLE OF CONTENTS

A PLACE IN SPACE

The Thanksgiving holiday is a day off work for most Americans. Yet on this Thanksgiving Day, researchers, including two Americans, buzz around a laboratory. Some conduct science experiments. Others unload supplies and repair a broken control panel. Finally, these researchers sit down to their Thanksgiving meal: turkey, green beans, yams, cornbread dressing, and mashed potatoes. There's just one difference— some of the food is pre-made in pouches. Other food is **dehydrated**. All the food floats. Where on Earth is this lab?

This lab is not on Earth at all. It's aboard the International Space Station (ISS), which **orbits** 240 miles (400 kilometers) above the Earth.

Designing a space-based structure like the ISS for living and working presents a major engineering challenge. How do you power the lab when you can't just call the electric company? Where can you find air to breathe? And without a sewer, how do you get rid of waste flushed down the toilet?

Science in Space

*Sometimes there is no place like space when it comes to science. The ISS is the only place scientists can study the effects of **microgravity** on the human body. They also examine how near-weightless conditions affect plants. These experiments could pave the way for future trips to Mars.*

SPACE STATIONS THROUGH TIME

ISSengineers are not the first to grapple with these issues. The Soviet Union's bus-sized Salyut became the world's first space station in 1971. Over the next decade, the Soviets launched six more space stations, which were home to astronauts from Bulgaria to Cuba and Vietnam. On Oct. 2, 1985, Soviet astronauts aboard Salyut 7, known as **cosmonauts**, set a record for the most days in space: 237 days.

An artist's concept illustrating an Apollo-type spacecraft (left) about to dock with a Soviet Soyuz-type spacecraft.

A Place of Peace

U.S. and Soviet astronauts first worked together in space in July 1975. A U.S. Apollo and Soviet Soyuz spacecraft came together in space, and the crews spent almost two days together. It paved the way for the ISS, which involves the cooperation of many countries.

In 1973, the United States launched its single-module Skylab space station. Over the next two years, three different astronaut crews lived inside and conducted experiments.

1973 Skylab

China's Space Station

Russia and the U.S. are not the only countries to launch space stations. The Chinese launched the Tiangong 1 space station in September 2011. In 2016, it launched Tiangong 2. Chinese "taikonauts" recently spent 30 days aboard the station.

The Soviets launched the first part of a far more complex space station, Mir, in 1986. Over a ten-year period, Soyuz spacecraft launched five more pieces with science equipment. Cosmonauts connected them together during spacewalks. In the end, Mir looked like six school buses stuck together, according to one visiting astronaut. Mir circled the Earth for 15 years.

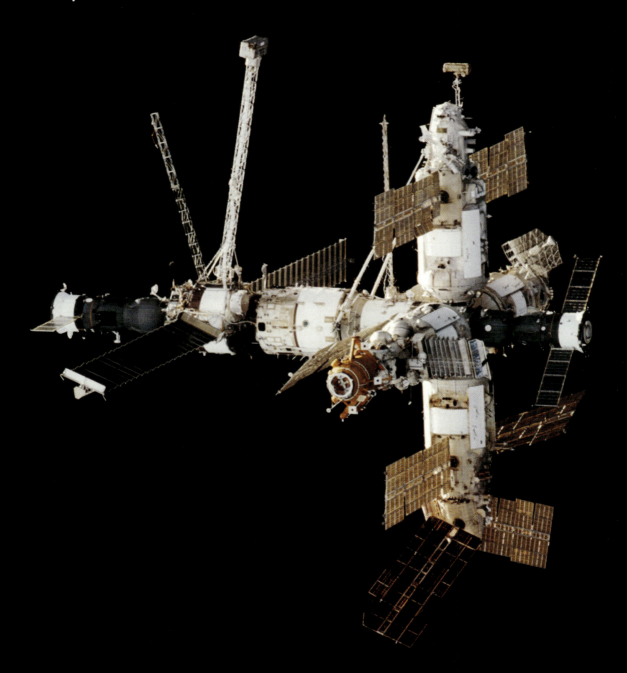

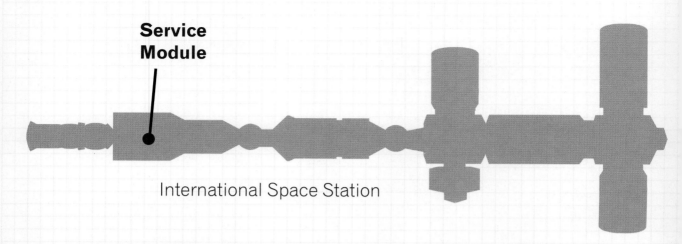

Service Module

International Space Station

PLACES TO LIVE AND WORK

The ISS has a lot in common with your house. It includes places to sleep, eat, and work. Yet designing such structures for space creates lots of challenges.

On Earth, buildings are often rectangular. Aboard the ISS, labs and living spaces take the shape of cylinders and spheres. These shapes reduce **stress** on the structure. The **atmosphere** inside the ISS is under great pressure compared to space around it, just like soda in a can. The atmosphere pushes out on the structure. Cylinders and spheres allow the atmosphere to exert pressure evenly, preventing weak spots. That's why soda cans are cylinders too.

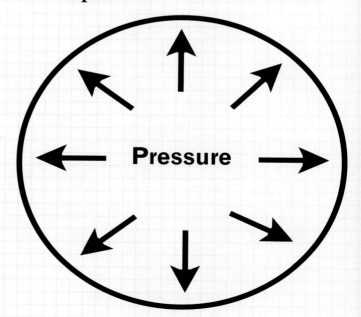

Pressure

Sleeping and Eating in Space

Ready to sleep? On the ISS, you sleep in a special sleeping bag anchored in place. You can position yourself any which way. Since you float, there's no feeling of lying down.

In the kitchen, forget about playing with pots and pans. Most of your food comes in pouches ready to eat. For others, you just add water. Yum!

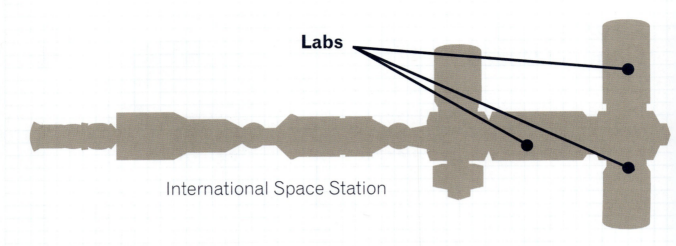

Labs

International Space Station

Conducting science in space has its own considerations. Astronauts don't peer through microscopes on tables or mix chemicals out in the open. Instead, experiments are housed in refrigerator-sized racks that line the walls, floor, and ceiling. Each rack has all the equipment required for its experiments. All racks are the same size, meaning science experiments can easily be swapped in and out.

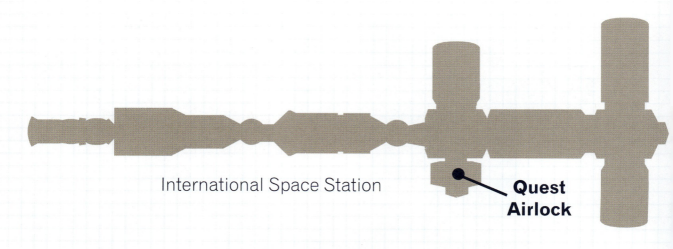

International Space Station

Quest Airlock

At home, you might have an entryway where you stash your boots or hang your backpack. On the ISS, that entryway is the Quest Airlock. Unlike your house, Quest has two doors, one to the outside and one to the rest of the ISS.

Astronauts use airlocks during spacewalks. After the door to the ISS is closed, the airlock's air pressure is lowered so its atmosphere is more like the space outside. Astronauts breathe in pure oxygen. After equipping themselves in special spacesuits, the outside door can be opened.

ISS Spacesuits

*The ISS spacewalking suits are known as Extravehicular Mobility Units or EMUs. They are like mini spaceships. They protect astronauts from harmful solar **radiation** and space debris. They also provide air for astronauts to breathe.*

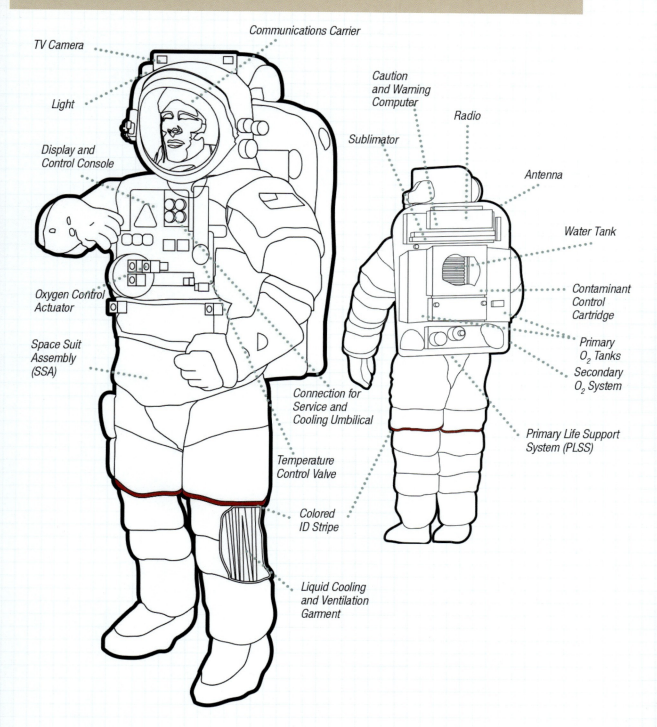

TV Camera

Communications Carrier

Light

Caution and Warning Computer

Radio

Display and Control Console

Sublimator

Antenna

Water Tank

Oxygen Control Actuator

Contaminant Control Cartridge

Space Suit Assembly (SSA)

Primary O₂ Tanks

Secondary O₂ System

Connection for Service and Cooling Umbilical

Temperature Control Valve

Colored ID Stripe

Primary Life Support System (PLSS)

Liquid Cooling and Ventilation Garment

Your home may have an attached garage. On the ISS, these garages are docking ports, special places where spaceships can attach. On Earth, most garages easily fit cars and trucks of every size. On the ISS, docking ports must have just the right connector to fit each type of visiting spaceship. This allows the spaceships to dock to the ISS automatically without help from the space station crew.

The truss serves as the backbone of the ISS. It's made of triangles and beams, much like skyscrapers or bridges on Earth. These make the truss strong and sturdy.

The truss serves as a spot to mount solar panels needed to make electricity. It also holds radiators that help keep the ISS at just the right temperature. Finally, all the utility lines that carry electricity, heating, and cooling run through the truss to different parts of the ISS.

21

INSIDE THE WALLS

If you could peel back the walls of the ISS, you'd find its inner workings are even more unusual. Your house probably has cables connecting it to the power grid. So does the ISS.

On Earth, the electric company sends your home power this way. There's no electric company in space though, so the ISS must make its own power. Solar panels soak up the sun's energy and convert it to electricity. Batteries store power for use at night.

Solar Power by the Numbers

The ISS can generate enough power to light up 40 homes. Its solar panels have a quarter million solar cells and take up half the space of a football field. Eight miles (12.9 kilometers) of wire carry electricity throughout the ISS.

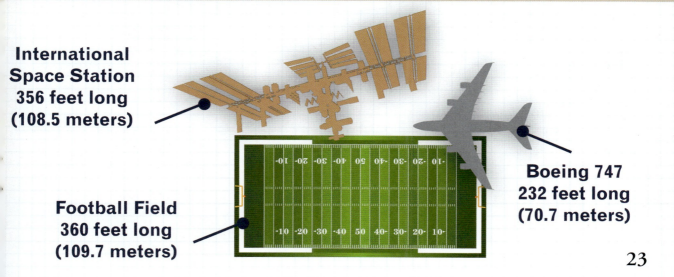

International Space Station 356 feet long (108.5 meters)

Boeing 747 232 feet long (70.7 meters)

Football Field 360 feet long (109.7 meters)

23

On Earth, you flush the toilet and wastewater flows from your house to a water treatment plant. But what happens on the ISS with no treatment plant in sight? The ISS has its own.

Since spaceships must carry water supplies to the ISS, the ISS is designed to recycle as much water as possible. The water system turns pee into drinkable water. It also takes water vapor astronauts breathe out and transforms that into drinking water too.

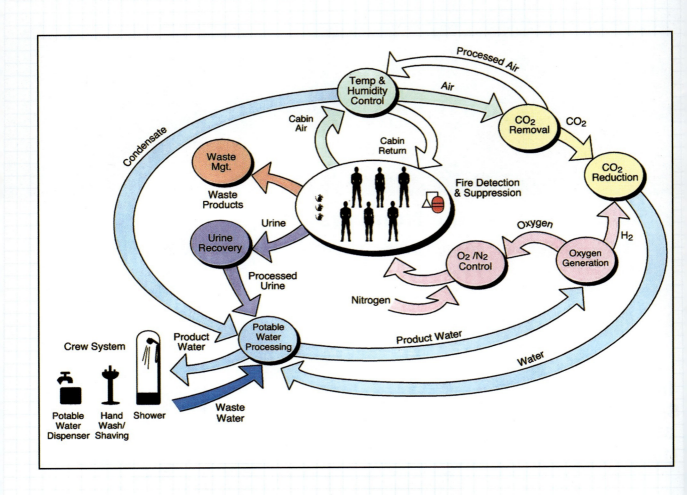

Toilet Training

ISS toilets look different from those on Earth. Water and waste would float out of a normal toilet bowl. The ISS toilet uses small openings and suction to whisk waste away. There are different places for pee and poop too. Getting the hang of it takes hours of training.

On Earth, engineers must design buildings with enough **insulation** to keep you warm and cool. Space structures must do more than protect you from the weather though. They also must protect astronauts from tiny **meteorites** and bits of space trash. Traveling at high speeds, these can rip holes in the ISS. The ISS has special shielding and curtains that act like a bullet-proof vest. This also protects astronauts from the sun's harmful radiation.

Radiation Risks

The Earth's atmosphere acts as a blanket, protecting you from the sun's harmful radiation. If your body gets too much radiation, you could get a sunburn or even cancer. The ISS floats above Earth's atmosphere. Without radiation shields, astronauts would be at risk.

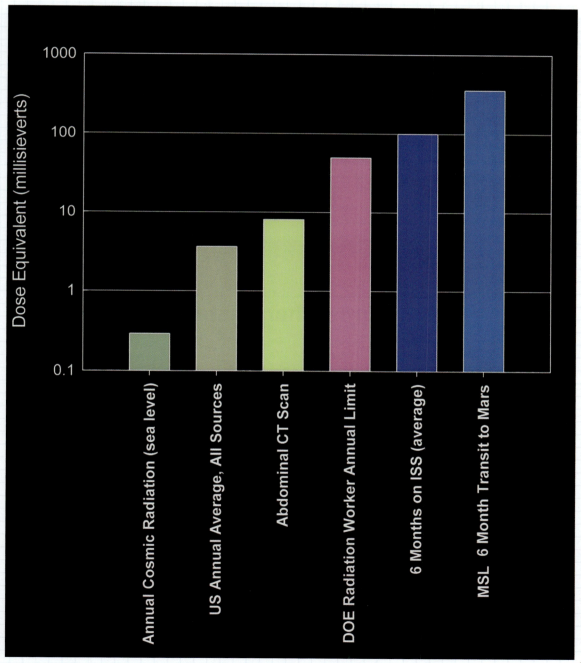

Your home's thermostat keeps you cool in summer and warm in winter, but it doesn't have to make sure you have enough oxygen to breathe. After all, air is all around. Not so in space! Astronauts on the ISS need a constant supply of fresh air. The environmental control system cleans carbon dioxide—the air you breathe out—from the air. It also makes sure astronauts have enough oxygen to breathe.

Home Thermostat

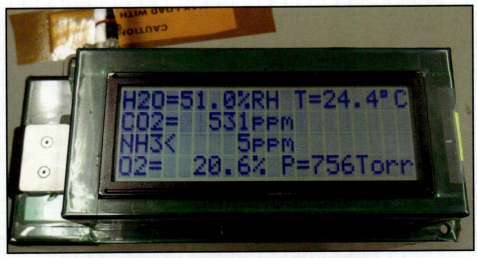

ISS Multi Gas Monitor

OXYGEN LEVELS AT ALTITUDE

FEET/METERS	LEVELS
30,000 feet / 9,144 meters	32%
15,000 feet / 4,572 meters	58%
5,000 feet / 1,524 meters	84%
Sea Level	100%

In some ways, the ISS has more in common with a car or plane than a house. It has **GPS** and antennas so it knows its position. Gyros help hold the ISS's position so it doesn't tumble. Thrusters boost the ISS and keep it from being pulled back to Earth.

Astronauts on the ISS need more than phones and email to communicate with people on Earth. Satellites carry audio, video, and data between the ISS and mission control.

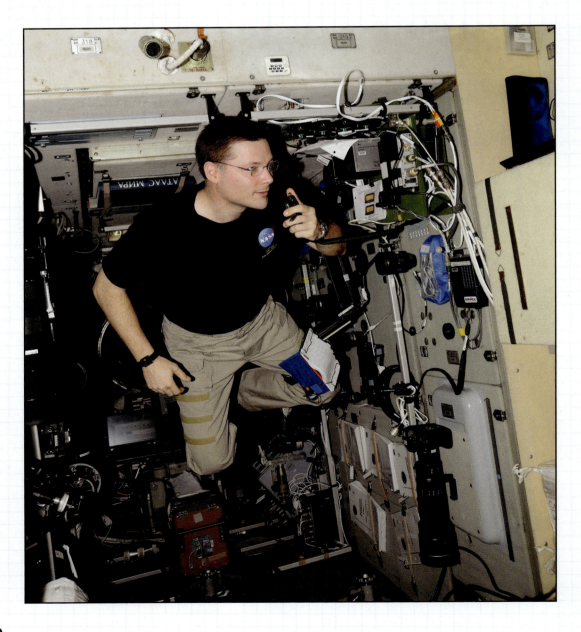

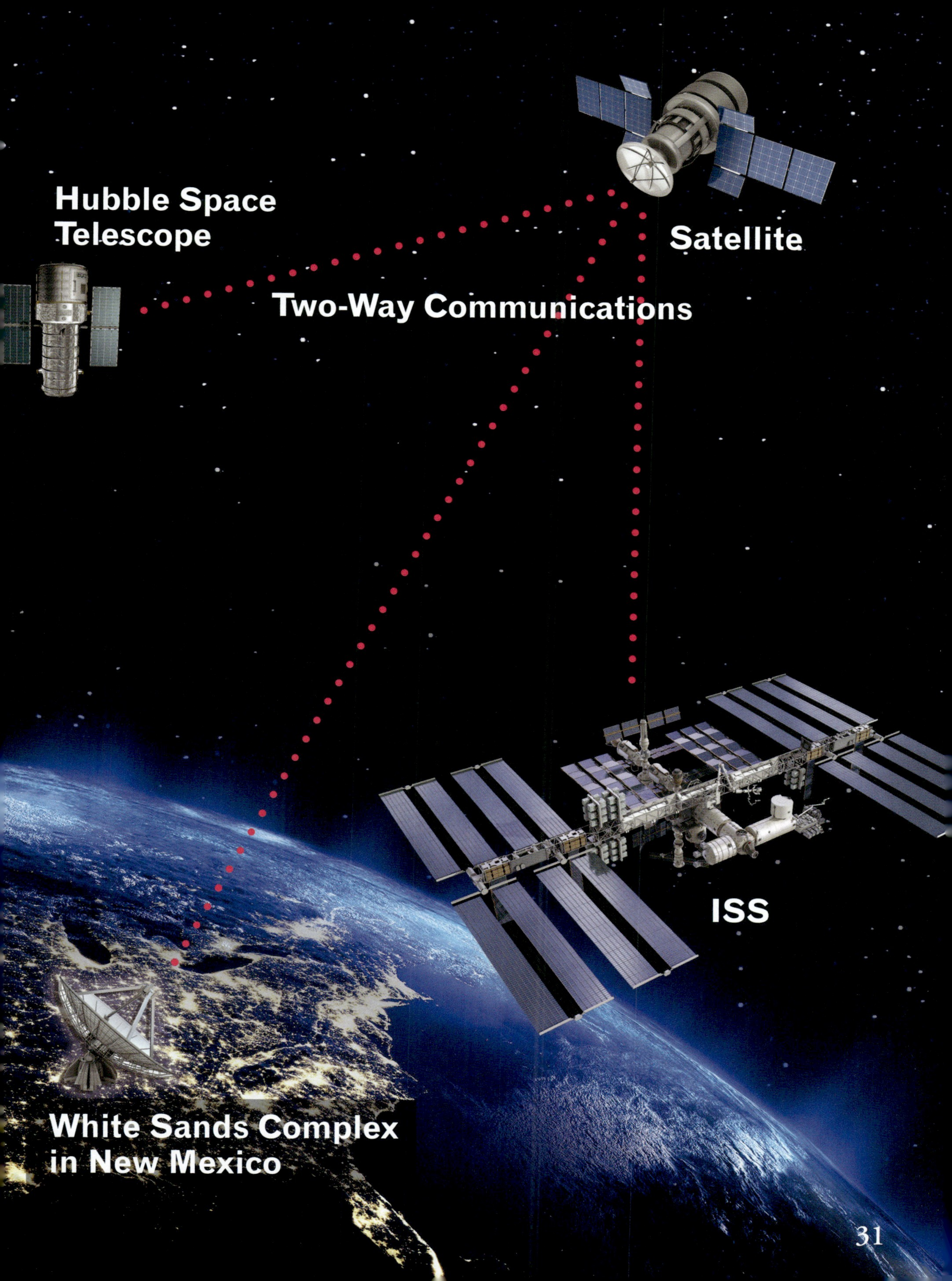

Hubble Space Telescope

Satellite

Two-Way Communications

ISS

White Sands Complex in New Mexico

31

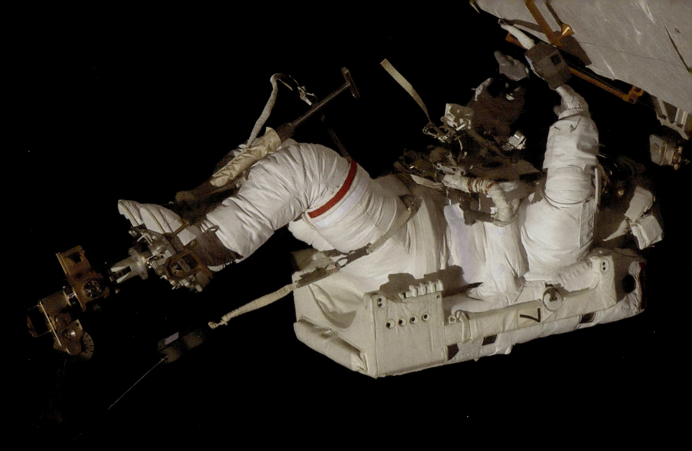

SOME ASSEMBLY REQUIRED

The ISS is the size of a football field. How did it get into space? Some assembly was required. Each piece was built on the ground and carried into space by Russian and U.S. spacecraft. Astronauts connected the pieces during spacewalks. Assembling the entire ISS took 13 years. Astronauts from around the world are scheduled to live on the ISS until at least 2020.

ISS Configuration

As of April 2016

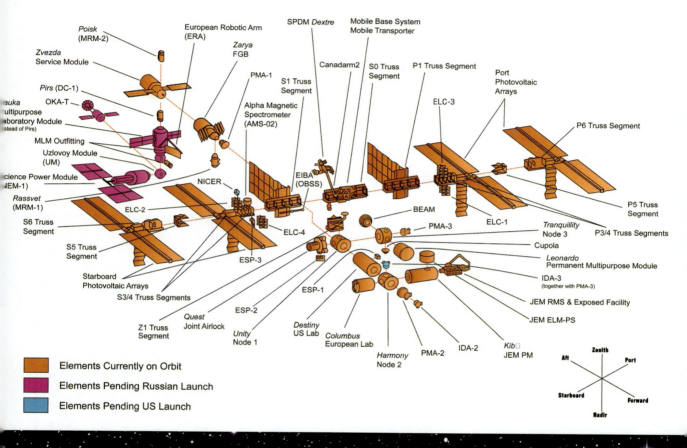

Poisk (MRM-2)

Zvezda Service Module

Pirs (DC-1)

Nauka Multipurpose Laboratory Module (instead of Pirs)

OKA-T

MLM Outfitting

Uzlovoy Module (UM)

Science Power Module (NEM-1)

Rassvet (MRM-1)

S6 Truss Segment

ELC-2

S5 Truss Segment

Starboard Photovoltaic Arrays

S3/4 Truss Segments

Z1 Truss Segment

Quest Joint Airlock

ESP-2

ESP-3

ELC-4

NICER

European Robotic Arm (ERA)

Zarya FGB

PMA-1

Alpha Magnetic Spectrometer (AMS-02)

S1 Truss Segment

SPDM Dextre

Canadarm2

EIBA (OBSS)

S0 Truss Segment

Mobile Base System Mobile Transporter

P1 Truss Segment

ELC-3

Port Photovoltaic Arrays

P6 Truss Segment

P5 Truss Segment

P3/4 Truss Segments

BEAM

PMA-3

ELC-1

Tranquillity Node 3

Cupola

Leonardo Permanent Multipurpose Module

IDA-3 (together with PMA-3)

JEM RMS & Exposed Facility

JEM ELM-PS

Kibō JEM PM

IDA-2

PMA-2

Columbus European Lab

Harmony Node 2

Destiny US Lab

Unity Node 1

ESP-1

Zenith
Aft
Port
Starboard
Forward
Nadir

	Elements Currently on Orbit
	Elements Pending Russian Launch
	Elements Pending US Launch

Starlight, Star Bright

The ISS is one of the brightest objects in the sky. It can be hard to spot though, since it hurtles overhead at 17,500 miles (28,163.52 kilometers) per hour. If you miss it, just wait three days and you'll get another chance.

In designing the ISS, engineers had to work within certain guidelines. U.S. and Russian spacecraft had to be able to carry each piece to space. Each element had to fit inside the spacecraft. The Space Shuttle's cargo space, called the payload bay, measured 60 by 15 feet (18.3 x 4.6 meters). Pieces also had be light enough to be lifted into space.

Assembling the ISS took 36 U.S. Space Shuttle flights and five Russian launches.

Payload Bay

Space shuttle Atlantis,
October 3, 1985

Once pieces reached orbit, astronauts conducted 160 spacewalks to hook them together. Much like construction workers on Earth, astronauts connected electrical wires and water lines between ISS pieces.

Regular power drills and screwdrivers don't cut it in space though. Astronauts use special tools that can stand up to extreme hot and cold. Tools are specially designed so astronauts can use them while wearing bulky spacesuit gloves.

Canadarm

Canadian robotic arms served as cranes to lift each new piece into place. Astronauts control the ISS's Canadarm from inside the station. It slides along a railway-like system so it can be positioned in just the right spot.

Keeping the ISS in good working order is an ongoing process. Sometimes things break and need repair. The ISS carries lots of spare parts for just this kind of situation since it can take months for spacecraft to arrive with new parts. Now the ISS crew is experimenting with 3-D printers. Engineers can send directions for new parts to the printer from Earth. The printer prints thin layers of plastic to create what's needed.

Robot Helper

NASA also is experimenting with Robonaut, a robot helper that lives on the ISS. Someday soon he may do jobs that are too dirty, dangerous, or just plain boring. These may include spacewalks.

FUTURE OF THE ISS

Though it was only designed to last until 2020, the ISS will continue to operate as an orbiting laboratory until at least 2024.

When the ISS's life ends, it will fall to Earth. First, astronauts will leave the station. Then the U.S. and Russia will use cargo spacecraft to guide the ISS into a safe position. Over time, without boosts to keep it in orbit, Earth's gravity will pull the ISS toward it. The empty spaceship likely will land in an ocean.

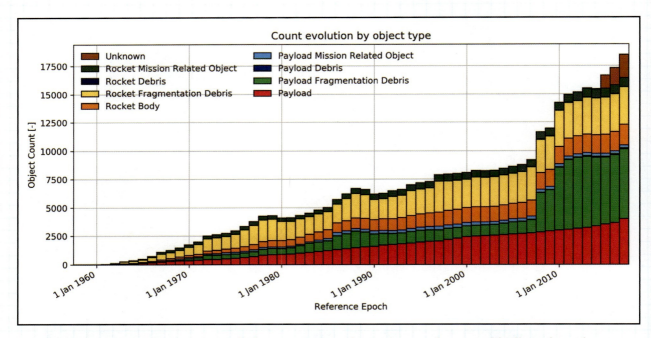

In 2017, space agencies counted almost 20,000 objects bigger than a softball circling the Earth. About 1,000 objects are satellites. The rest is space trash. At high speeds, space trash can damage spacecraft.

Mir Returns to Earth

When Russian Space Station Mir fell to Earth, other space agencies watched carefully. In March 2001, Mir entered the Earth's atmosphere. Solar panels and other pieces ripped off before the remains fell into the South Pacific.

When the ISS returns to Earth, it won't be the end of space stations. Russia has said it may remove some ISS pieces and reuse them to build a new space station. The Russian Orbital Station will be smaller than the ISS, at least at first.

Some space companies propose building a space station that orbits Mars. This could serve as a base station for exploring the Red Planet. Such a project would create a new set of engineering challenges.

Fresh food is grown on the ISS. Crew members ate half of the first harvest, then sent the rest back to Earth to be studied. Food growing technology is important for future manned missions deeper in the solar system, such as Mars.

The journey to Mars takes about nine months. And a trip to Mars is only possible every 26 months, when Mars and Earth are lined up properly. There's no quick way to get supplies restocked. Fresh food would need to be grown. Engineers, scientists, and others are discovering ways to make this possible.

SPACE POTTY PRO

NASA's Scott Weinstein spends a lot of time in the bathroom, but not just any bathroom. Weinstein works in an Earth-based space toilet at NASA's Johnson Space Center in Houston. His specialty: teaching astronauts how to go potty in space, which is a complicated process.

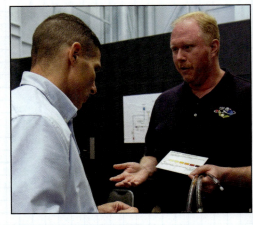

Scott Weinstein (right) trains astronaut Mike Hopkins (left) before his trip to space.

Weinstein's an engineer, but his official job title is "flight crew systems instructor." That means he trains astronauts how to do things in space that they would normally do at home. This includes going to the bathroom, cooking, and sleeping.

Weinstein shows astronauts how to turn on the toilet and ensure it's working before they do their business. He also instructs them on keeping themselves from floating away and cleaning up afterward with wet wipes.

Besides training astronauts before they launch, Weinstein sometimes works with them in space too. This is especially important if a piece of ISS equipment isn't working or if major housecleaning is underway. During these times, Weinstein sits at a special workstation in Houston's Mission Control so he can talk to astronauts and answer their questions.

Weinstein holds degrees in civil and environmental engineering, while many of his colleagues have aerospace engineering degrees. "It's really about the fundamentals," he says. Trainers must understand the challenges of the space environment—without having traveled there themselves.

TIMELINE

Jan. 25, 1984 – U.S. President Ronald Reagan calls for the construction of an international space station.

Nov. 20, 1998 – Russians launch first piece of ISS, known as Zarya.

Dec. 4, 1998 – First U.S. piece of the ISS, called Unity, launches aboard the Space Shuttle.

Nov. 2, 2000 – First crew makes the ISS its home. Crew includes U.S. astronaut Bill Shepherd and Russian cosmonauts Yuri Gidzenko and Sergei Krikalev.

Feb. 7, 2001 – U.S. Laboratory called Destiny launched to the ISS aboard STS-98. It is later designated a U.S. National Laboratory.

Feb. 7, 2008 – European laboratory, called Columbus, launched.

March 11, 2008 – First part of Japanese Kibo laboratory launched.

Oct. 10, 2008 – U.S. Astronaut Peggy Whitson launches into space, where she serves as first woman commander of the ISS.

July 21, 2011 – Space Shuttle lands after last ISS assembly mission; ISS construction is complete.

Oct. 8, 2012 – SpaceX launches its first resupply mission to the ISS; SpaceX is the first private company to carry experiments and supplies to the ISS for NASA.

March 2, 2016 – NASA astronaut Mark Kelly and Russian cosmonaut Mikhail Kornienko marked the longest mission to the ISS to date. The two men spent over a year in space as part of experiments to learn how humans might fare during long spaceflights. A trip to Mars would take about 30 months, for example.

May 16, 2016 – The ISS marks its 100,000th orbit around the Earth.

GLOSSARY

atmosphere (AT-muhs-feer): mixture of gases that surrounds a planet

cosmonauts (KAHZ-moh-nawts): Russian people who travel in space

dehydrated (dee-hye-dray-tid): with all the water removed

GPS (GPS): a system of satellites and devices that people use to find out where they are, or to get directions to a place; GPS is short for Global Positioning System

insulation (IN-suh-lay-shun): material that stops heat, electricity, or sound from escaping

meteorites (MEE-tee-uh-rites): pieces of rock from space that fall to Earth

microgravity (mye-kroh-GRAV-i-tee): very weak gravity

orbits (OR-bits): travels in a circular path around something

radiation (ray-dee-AY-shuhn): giving off energy in the form of light or heat

stress (stres): strain or pressure

INDEX

SHOW WHAT YOU KNOW

1. How did missions like *Apollo-Soyuz*, Skylab, and Mir pave the way for the International Space Station?

2. How many spacewalks did it take to build the ISS?

3. Using the graphics, how many laboratories does the ISS have?

4. Why are some ISS parts shaped like cylinders or spheres?

5. What will happen when the ISS's lifespan is over?

WEBSITES TO VISIT

www.nasa.gov/mission_pages/station/main/index.html

www.nasa.gov/mission_pages/station/research/ops/research_student.html

https://spotthestation.nasa.gov

ABOUT THE AUTHOR

Kirsten used to work with rocket scientists at NASA. Now she writes about rocket science — and just about any science — for kids. She is the author of more than 20 children's books about everything from special ops to SWAT teams and sloths. She lives near Los Angeles, California with her family. Learn more at kirsten-w-larson.com.

Meet The Author!
www.meetREMauthors.com

www.rourkeeducationalmedia.com

PHOTO CREDITS: Cover and title page: courtesy of NASA; p.17, 24: ©Reference Guide to the International Space; p.26: ©johan63/iStock; p.27: @Wiki; p.28: ©samiylenko/iStock; p.29, 31, 43: ©scibak/iStock; p.29: ©1xpert/iStock; p.31: ©1xpert/iStock, ©Madmaxer/iStock, ©jamesbenet/iStock, ©Andrey Prokhorov/iStock; p.40: courtesy of ESA.int; p.41: ©PaulFleet/iStock; p.43: ©Tokarsky/iStock; All other photos courtesy of NASA

Edited by: Keli Sipperley
Cover and interior design by: Kathy Walsh

Library of Congress PCN Data

International Space Station / Kirsten W. Larson
 (Engineering Wonders)
 ISBN 978-1-68342-389-8 (hard cover)
 ISBN 978-1-68342-459-8 (soft cover)
 ISBN 978-1-68342-555-7 (e-Book)
Library of Congress Control Number: 2017931280

Rourke Educational Media
Printed in the United States of America,
North Mankato, Minnesota